Bobby Otter
and the Blue Boat

by Margaret Burdick

A MAPLE FOREST STORY

Little, Brown and Company
Boston   Toronto

For Joanne and Charles

First Edition

Library of Congress Cataloging-in-Publication Data
Burdick, Margaret.
  Bobby Otter and the blue boat.

  Summary: Bobby Otter, one of the inhabitants of Maple Forest, tries to find something valuable enough to trade for the blue boat in Mr. Badger's store.
  [1. Otters—Fiction.   2. Boats and boating—Fiction]
I. Title.
PZ7.B91624Bo 1986   [E]   86-10403
ISBN 0-316-11616-5

Designed by Trisha Hanlon

WOR

Published simultaneously in Canada
by Little, Brown & Company (Canada) Limited

Printed in the United States of America

Bobby saw the new boat in the window of Badger's Trading Post. It was blue and had a big sail. The little card beside it read, FOR TRADE—MADE BY MR. BEAVER. "What will I be able to trade for that beautiful blue boat?" Bobby wondered.

He walked away and tried to imagine something of his, something from home. But he couldn't think of anything.

FOR TRADE
MADE BY
MR. BEAVER

The path through the Maple Forest was full of autumn leaves. Bobby thought it would be fun to slide on them down the hill and into the Silver Stream. *Whirr,* a tiny red leaf came spinning down. "These leaves are very pretty," Bobby thought. "I can trade them for the boat!" He carefully gathered the best red, yellow, and orange ones, and hurried back to Mr. Badger's.

"I'm sorry, Bobby," said Mr. Badger, "but I don't think Mr. Beaver will want leaves. I cannot trade the blue boat for them."

Bobby spread the bright colors across the counter. "I gave some like these to my mother once," he said, "and she liked them a lot."

"I'm sure she did," answered Mr. Badger. "But when winter comes they will turn brown and crumbly. Then Mr. Beaver will have nothing, and you will still have the blue boat."

"Oh, I see," said Bobby quietly, "not a good trade." He took the leaves and returned to the sliding hill.

That afternoon Bobby was back, carrying a big bundle of sticks. "Look, Mr. Badger! I've brought some delicious elm twigs. Mr. Beaver will love them!"

"Yes," agreed Mr. Badger. "These twigs will make a fine meal for Mr. Beaver. But he can enjoy them for only one night. You will enjoy the boat for many days and nights. It is not a fair trade. Here is a fresh fish for your twigs. That is a fair trade."

Bobby carried the fish home to his mother. When it was ready, the Otters ate it all up and licked their whiskers.

After dinner Father Otter settled back in his chair and closed his eyes. Bobby closed his eyes, too, and saw a shiny blue boat sailing away.

The next day Bobby was on the bank of the Silver
Stream, sliding down the leaves into the bubbling water,
when he noticed some pebbles shining in the riverbed.
In the water they looked just like sparkling jewels.
"These must be the prettiest things in the Maple Forest,"
thought Bobby. He scooped up the stones and ran to the
Trading Post.

But when he arrived, the stones had dried and were not shiny anymore.

"Yes, Bobby?" asked Mr. Badger.

Bobby knew he could not trade dull, dry stones for the shiny blue boat. He shook his head and left the Trading Post.

Bobby watched the sun set behind the trees of the
Maple Forest. He knew now that to get the blue boat
he would have to give Mr. Badger something that would
stay bright and beautiful and that Mr. Beaver could enjoy
for a long time. What could it be?

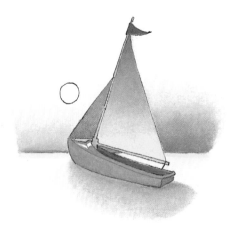

That night after Mother Otter had tucked him in,
Bobby dreamed of the blue boat. It drifted across a
golden sunset, its sails the colors of autumn leaves, and
the rising moon shone like a smooth, round pebble. . . .

Bobby opened his eyes wide. It was morning, and he had something to do. He got out his paint box, a jar of water, and some special paper. He closed his eyes and remembered for just a minute. Then, wetting his brush, he spread all the colors of sunset in the Maple Forest over the paper. He filled his picture with leaves and twigs and shining pebbles.

Bobby ran through the Maple Forest and got to the
Trading Post just as Mr. Badger was opening the door.

"Bobby, that is a wonderful painting," said Mr. Badger. "I will trade the blue boat for it. It will give Mr. Beaver many days of pleasure."

And it did.